Pepper's Purple Heart

A Veterans Day Story

Written and Illustrated
by
Heather French Henry

To Judy —
All my love!
Heather French Henry
Miss America 2000

AAP Publishing, Inc.
Woodland Hills, California

Design by Jaye Oliver

Published by CB Publishing, Inc.,
21900 Marylee Street, #290, Woodland Hills, CA 91367
Printed in the United States of America

Publisher's Cataloging-in-Publication Data

Henry, Heather French.

　　Pepper's Purple Heart : a Veterans Day story /
written and illustrated by Heather French Henry.
-- 1st ed. -- Woodland Hills, Calif. : CB Publishing,
2004.

　　　p. ; cm.
　　(Claire's holiday adventures)

　　　ISBN: 0-9706341-0-2
　　　0-9706341-1-0 (pbk.)

　　　1. Veterans Day--United States--Juvenile
fiction. 2. Armistice Day--United States--
Juvenile fiction. 3. Holidays--United States--
Juvenile fiction. 4. Purple Heart--Juvenile
fiction. 5. Puppies--Juvenile fiction. I. Title.

PZ7 .H467 2004　　　　　2003107862
[E]--dc21　　　　　　　　0310

10 9 8 7 6 5 4 3 2

Claire woke up with the sun licking her face. Her shaggy puppy, Pepper, jumped on the bed and covered her with kisses.

Suddenly Pepper's ears shot straight up and Claire heard a *tap-tap* at the window.

It was her best friend, Robbie, out in the yard with his nose squished against the glass.

"Get up, lazybones," Robbie called. He wore his dad's army helmet and raised his hand in a salute. Propping a stick against his shoulder he marched around the yard.

Laughing, Claire threw back the covers and jumped out of bed.

"Who's out there?" Claire's mom stared out the window.

"It's just Robbie."

Mom frowned. "I don't like it when you play soldiers."

"Did you forget, Mom? We're going to march in a parade for soldiers. It's Veterans Day."

Claire rolled with Pepper on the bed. "Pepper gets
to march, too. But first we're going to save her from the
enemy—like Robbie's dad did with real soldiers in Viet-raq."

Mom smiled. "He was in Iraq, not Vietnam.
They are different countries, dear."

Claire dressed in a dark green T-shirt, brown pants, and her rescue shoes. Glancing in the mirror, she frowned. "These aren't exactly army clothes."

"They are good enough for a backyard adventure," said Mom.

"I guess so," Claire sighed. "Mom, where did Dad fight?"

"He didn't. He was in the Coast Guard, protecting our shores. Remember that picture of him on a boat in a terrible storm?"

"Oh, yes." Claire was so deep in thought she did not notice that Pepper had snatched a bandanna from the night-table drawer.

"This will be Pepper's uniform," said Claire, tying the bandanna around her pup's neck. Pepper squirmed, pulling at her new collar.

"Just make sure she stays in the yard," Mom warned. "You know she loves to chase cars."

Claire rolled her eyes. "Oh, Mom, she'll be fine." The little girl tapped her chest with her thumb. "Pepper always does what I say."

After breakfast, Claire tied Pepper under the picnic table and dashed over to join Robbie. Pepper poked her nose between the table legs, looking very sad.

The two eight-year-olds then dropped to the ground and crawled on their bellies among the bushes. Hiding behind a hedge, they planned their rescue mission.

"Are we in Iraq or Vietnam?" whispered Claire.

"Hmm," thought Robbie. "Dad says Iraq is a desert and Vietnam is a jungle." He pushed away a clump of scratchy leaves. "This must be Vietnam."

Claire imagined the steamy jungle and pretended to swat a bug. "Ugh, the jungle insects are so bad. I hope Sergeant Pepper is all right. We've got to save her . . . *now!*"

Robbie wiped his face, leaving a streak of dirt across his forehead. "We won't let her get captured by the enemy. We'll zoom in by helicopter and rescue her before they come."

Claire and Robbie crept quickly onto the grass and stood up. They slapped each other's palms in a high five and together yelled, "Go!"

The two little soldiers ran past the back door; they ran past Claire's Mom hanging laundry on the side of the house, and straight to the fence in the front yard. They scooted out the front gate, dashed around the neighbor's tree, and charged back into the yard. Robbie swung his stick. Claire spread her arms as if she had wings. Pepper yipped and pulled on the leash.

Robbie hollered into his hand-radio, "Coming in for a landing."

"Roger that, sir," Claire hissed. She skidded to a stop and Robbie tumbled into her.

After making sure the coast was clear, Claire and Robbie hopped onto the picnic bench for the final stage of the mission. Holding hands, they counted, "One, two, three!" and jumped. Robbie leapt so high that his helmet flew off and he landed with a thud. "Ouch!" he squealed as he rolled onto his stick.

Claire lost her balance and fell to her knees. Giggling, she picked herself up and rushed toward Pepper.

"Hurry, the enemy is coming!" Robbie shouted.

Sergeant Pepper shimmied feverishly on her back while Claire undid the leash. Then the rascal pup darted out from under the picnic table and raced around the yard.

"Stop, Pepper," Claire ordered. But the puppy did not stop. She bounded past the back door, under the laundry blowing in the wind, directly to the fence, and out the front gate.

"Oops," said Robbie.

"Mom, help!" yelled Claire.

Mom asked what was wrong, but Claire was so scared she couldn't talk. All she could do was point toward the street.

A moment later, they heard the screech of tires and Pepper's miserable yelp.

Claire, Robbie, and Mom were horrified to find that Pepper had been hit by a car.

The driver knelt beside the puppy. Claire's neighbor, Mr. Jones, stood close by, leaning on his cane.

Unable to move her back leg, Pepper whined in pain. Claire and Robbie started to cry, too.

"I'm so sorry," said the woman. "She rushed in front of me before I could stop."

Neighbors watched from their yards. Kids got off their bikes to stare.

"Don't worry," called out Mr. Jones. "She's just got a bump on her leg. She's going to be okay."

"I'll take Pepper to the veterinary clinic," said Mom. "Mr. Jones, can you watch these little soldiers while I'm gone?"

"I'd be delighted." Mr. Jones grinned. "I know all about soldiers."

Claire, Robbie, and Mr. Jones waved good-bye to Mom and went next door. As Claire slumped in a wicker chair on the porch, Mr. Jones brought out a tray of milk and cookies. Robbie snatched a cookie and sat on the steps.

Handing his neighbor a glass of cold milk, Mr. Jones said gently, "Don't feel bad, Claire."

"My puppy got too excited. She got hurt because I didn't listen to Mom." Another tear rolled down her cheek. "Now Sergeant Pepper won't be able to march in the parade." She took a noisy gulp of milk.

"Rescue missions are always dangerous." Mr. Jones sat next to her and patted her arm. "Let's wait and see what the medic says about that leg."

Claire bolted upright, looking straight at him. "You seem to really know about these things. Are you a veteran?"

"Yes, I was a marine in Vietnam." Mr. Jones pulled thoughtfully on his mustache. "It was a hard war and I was taken prisoner."

"Do all veterans fight in wars?" Robbie grabbed two more cookies from the plate.

"No, but all people who served in the military are veterans," replied Mr. Jones, resting his chin on his cane. "Today, we'll be marching with folks from the Army, the Navy, the Air Force, the Marines, and the Coast Guard."

"Why do you walk with that?" Robbie pointed at Mr. Jones's cane.

"I got wounded in the leg, just like Sergeant Pepper."

Claire pinched up her face. "Did it hurt a lot?"

"Yes, at first. Now, I just limp a little."

He handed the cane to Robbie.

"Try walking with it."

Robbie leaned on the smooth handle then hobbled down the steps.

"I'm going to be a soldier, too." Robbie tapped on his helmet.

"It's important to serve your country, Robbie. But you have to be very alert," warned Mr. Jones.

Robbie teetered on one foot and spun around on the cane. Tumbling off the bottom step, he landed in a heap on the grass. His shirtsleeve had ripped at the seam. "I guess I'm not quite ready to be a soldier."

Mr. Jones laughed and said, "First you have to go through Basic Training, Private Robbie."

"I don't think I can be a soldier," Claire said. "I'm a girl."

"Of course you can. There are lots of women in the military." Mr. Jones reached into his shirt pocket and pulled out two photographs. He handed Claire a picture of a woman in uniform. "Let me tell you a little story. After I came out of the prison camp, I went to an army hospital. I was sick with fever." Claire passed the picture to Robbie. "My leg was very sore, but an army nurse taught me to walk again. I thought she was an angel. Guess what?"

"What?" asked the two children.

"I married her!"

Robbie looked at the photograph and nodded. "Women soldiers are always nurses."

"No, no!" chuckled Mr. Jones. He pushed the plate of cookies closer to the children and balanced against it a picture of a family. "The woman with the medals is my daughter. She was in the Iraq war like your dad, Robbie. Now she's a sergeant. She trains men and women to be good soldiers."

Claire stared at the picture and exclaimed, "She has children. Even moms can be soldiers!"

Claire, Robbie, and Mr. Jones heard a car horn honk out front. There was Mom, in the driver's seat, and Pepper, peeking out the window. The pup barked when she saw them.

As Mom carried Pepper to the porch, Claire spotted a big bandage on her back leg. She looked up at her mom, with worried eyes.

"She has a bad bruise but she's going to be fine," Mom reassured her.

Claire scratched her puppy's ears. Hanging her head, she said, "Mom, I'm sorry I didn't listen to you. I wasn't a good soldier on Veterans Day."

"It's okay, Claire. You've learned the hard way." Mom smiled and hugged her little girl. "I saw lots of people gathering downtown. Robbie, your dad and Claire's dad are hanging flags on the streetlights. It's almost time to march."

Claire looked down at her dirty shirt. "I can't march in my messy play clothes."
Robbie grabbed his helmet from the table. "I can wear my dad's helmet. But my sleeve is ripped."

Mr. Jones held up his hand and said, "I have the perfect clothes for this parade."

Mr. Jones went in the house and returned a few minutes later with camouflage shirts for Claire and Robbie. The name *Jones* was stitched on the pockets. "I wore these when I was in Vietnam," he explained.

Claire marveled at his fine uniform coat with four stars decorating each shoulder. "What are those stars?" she wondered aloud.

"After Vietnam, I became a four-star general in the United States Marine Corps."

She stood at attention. "Claire reporting for duty, sir." Pepper barked. "And my first order, Sergeant Pepper, is to take better care of you."

Mr. Jones removed the plate of cookies from the table and opened a little box. Three shiny medals lay on a velvet pad. He held up one attached to a yellow, red, and green ribbon. "I got this for serving in Vietnam." He held up another, engraved with an eagle and fastened to a black ribbon with red, white, and blue stripes. "This is a Prisoner of War medal." Lifting the third medal, Mr. Jones announced, "And this one is for Pepper. Every wounded soldier gets a Purple Heart." He pinned it to Pepper's bandanna.

"I know I'm not ready to be a real soldier, General Jones, but I wish I could do something to serve our country," said Robbie.

"You can. There's a special hospital for veterans. I go twice a week to serve meals. Come with me. They'd love to meet you."

"I would like that," Robbie said.

Claire jumped up and down. "Let's go *now* . . . Well, let's go after we take care of Pepper."

"Isn't it time to get ready for the parade?" asked Robbie. "I want to march with my dad and General Jones." He leaned over and hugged Claire's furry puppy. "Too bad Sergeant Pepper can't come."

"I'm under orders not to leave her behind. There must be some way Pepper can march with us. Right, Mom?" asked Claire. "After all, she's a veteran of the Backyard Rescue Mission."

Mom stroked Pepper's head and thought for a minute. Then she grinned and said, "I know just what to do."

A Brief History of Veterans Day

Veterans Day honors all men and women who have served in the armed forces of the United States. It began as Armistice Day (*armistice* means truce) to commemorate the end of World War I in November 1918, honoring the soldiers lost in the war. In 1921, France placed a tomb for unknown soldiers in the Arc de Triomphe, England placed one in Westminster Abbey, and the United States placed one at Arlington National Cemetery.

However, the truce between nations did not last, so in 1954 the United States changed the name to Veterans Day. The Tomb of the Unknowns at Arlington has a crypt for unknown soldiers who fought in World War I, World War II, Korea, and Vietnam.

Veterans Day is celebrated every year on the eleventh hour of the eleventh day of the eleventh month. The president places a wreath on the tomb and a color guard fires rifles to "present arms" in tribute to lost soldiers. A soldier guards the tomb day and night.